A First Time Book®

The Berenstain Bears and the Papa's Day Surprise

Stan & Jan Berenstain

Random House New York

 Published in the United States by Random House Children's Books, a division of Random House, Inc., New York.
Random House and the colophon are registered trademarks of Random House, Inc.
First Time Books and the colophon are registered trademarks of Berenstain Enterprises, Inc.
randomhouse.com/kids BerenstainBears.com
Library of Congress Cataloging-in-Publication Data
Berenstain, Stan. The Berenstain Bears and the Papa's Day surprise / Stan and Jan Berenstain.
p. cm. — (A first time book)
Summary: Papa Bear makes it clear to his family that he does not believe in celebrating Father's Day, then changes his opinion but fears it may be too late for any special treatment.
ISBN 978-0-375-81129-6 (trade) — ISBN 978-0-375-91129-3 (lib. bdg.) — ISBN 978-0-375-98257-6 (ebook)
[1. Father's Day—Fiction. 2. Bears—Fiction.] I. Title: Papa's Day surprise. II. Berenstain, Jan. III. Title.
PZ7.B4483 Bejok 2003 [E]—dc21 2002015698
Printed in the United States of America 30 29 28 27 26 25 24 23 22 21 20 19 18 17 16

Papa Bear is a bear of many opinions. He has opinions about all sorts of things. He has an opinion about the best way to fell trees.

He has an opinion about
predicting the weather.

He has an opinion about
the best kind of honey.

And though in his opinion, Mother's Day is a fine and proper holiday and a worthy tribute to the institution of motherhood, he didn't think much of Father's Day.

“That’s fine with us,” said Mama. “It’s a busy time for me with the quilting bee coming up. And with the school year ending, the cubs are going to be pretty busy, too.”

“Then it’s agreed,” said Papa. “We are not going to make a fuss about Father’s Day.”

A few days later, Papa was fixing a creaky front step, Mama was working on her tulip bed, and Baby Honey Bear was playing on the grass. Above their heads a pair of robins was hard at work building a nest.

"The fuss about Father's Day is a lot of nonsense," said Papa. "Look at that daddy robin helping that mama robin build a nest. He doesn't need to have a fuss made over him. He's happy to do his job building the nest, sitting on the eggs when the time comes, and digging up worms when the chicks hatch. That daddy robin doesn't need a special day, and neither do I."

"Yes, dear," said Mama.

Papa was about to continue when he heard a noise in his shop. "Hey," he said, "there's somebody rooting around in my shop. If it's those pesky raccoons again, I'll . . ."

But it wasn't raccoons. It was Brother and Sister Bear.

"What are you two up to?" asked Papa.

"Er—we're just getting some stuff for a school project," said Brother.

"Er, that's right," said Sister, "a school project." Brother was holding a piece of the special paper that Papa used for his furniture designs. Sister was holding a roll of the paper Papa put down when he was painting.

"Okay," said Papa. "Just so it's got nothing to do with Father's Day. Is that clear?"

"Very clear," said the cubs.

But as Father's Day drew closer, talk about it was very much in the air—and *on* the air as well:

on the radio,

on television,

at the mall,

and just about everywhere else.

Just as the drip, drip, drip of water can wear away solid rock, the constant talk about Father's Day began to wear away Papa's opinion about Father's Day.

A couple of days before Father's Day, Mama and Papa were in the living room. Mama was putting the finishing touches on a quilt.

"You know," said Papa, "I think maybe I'm being a little selfish about Father's Day. It's a lot of nonsense, of course. But cubs are cubs, and if they want to make a little fuss about it . . ."

"Sorry, dear," said Mama. "I was counting stitches and didn't hear a word you were saying."

Then the phone rang and Mama picked it up. "Yes," she said, "this is she. Yes, Mrs. Bruin. It's all arranged. See you there. Goodbye."

"What was *that* about?" asked Papa.

"Er—just some quilting business," said Mama.

"By the way," said Papa, "where *are* the cubs?"

"They're over at Cousin Fred's working on a big scout project," said Mama.

"Oh," said Papa. "I thought they were working on a big *school* project."

"Er—that's right," said Mama. "It's a big school *and* scout project."

Papa would never have admitted it, but he was beginning to hope that Mama and the cubs wouldn't worry about his opinion regarding Father's Day. He even looked in drawers and closets for hidden presents.

But there weren't any.

Now it was the day before Father's Day. Papa was on his way to his shop when he noticed the daddy robin. Mama robin had laid the eggs and the daddy was sitting on them.

"Mr. Robin," said Papa, "I think Mama and the cubs are up to something. And I think I know what it is: It's Father's Day! They're going to surprise me."

Mr. Robin didn't say anything. He just sat there.

Papa knew what Mama and the cubs were doing. They were *pretending* to skip Father's Day. Well, two could play at that game. Tomorrow morning, when he woke up to breakfast in bed and lots of presents and cards on Father's Day, he would pretend to be surprised.

But the next morning he didn't have to pretend. He really *was* surprised! There was no breakfast in bed! There were no gifts and cards!

But wait a minute! What was that delicious smell coming up from the kitchen? It was his favorite food: French-fried honeycomb. There *was* going to be a Father's Day breakfast. It just wasn't going to be in bed.

But the French-fried honeycomb wasn't for him at all. Mama explained that it was a gift for the new family down the road.

Papa went out and sat on the front steps. The daddy robin flew by. He was carrying a worm to his newly hatched chicks.

"Happy Father's Day, Mr. Robin," said Papa. "For all the good it's going to do us."

At that moment Mama and the cubs came down the front steps.
"Where are you going?" asked Papa. "What about breakfast?"
"We're all going for brunch at the Grizzmore Grille."
"Huh?" said Papa.

"The Grizzmore Grille, please," said the cubs as they piled into the car.

When they arrived, folks were lined up at the entrance.

"Look!" said Papa. "There's a sign over the door that says, 'Welcome, Dads'!"

"So there is!" said Mama with a big grin.

There was a much bigger sign inside. It said, *"Welcome to the Papa's Day Surprise."* It was painted on the roll of paper the cubs had gotten for the "school project." And there was a stage with a long table.

"Go ahead, Papa," said the cubs. "Up on the stage with the other papas."

He found a chair with his name on it at the long table. Other papas were on the stage with him: Lizzy Bruin's papa, Cousin Fred's papa, even Too-Tall's papa. Other papas filled the seats. And the food! All Papa's favorites: French-fried honeycomb, honey-cured salmon, honeyed squash.

WELCOME TO THE PAPA'S DAY SURPRISE

Someone began to speak. It was Mayor Honeypot. "And now we shall hear from those who put this wonderful surprise together. Our first speakers will be Brother and Sister Bear."

Brother and Sister cleared their throats and read a poem. It was on the special paper they had taken from Papa's shop.

To the best Papa Bear
in the whole wide world:
You are big and strong and true.
And no matter what we do,
we know we can depend on you.
You cheer us on when we are glad.
You cheer us up when we are sad.
You are always there for us,
to help, advise, and care for us.
Happy Father's Day!

Papa looked out over the audience. But he could hardly see. His eyes were misty and he had a lump in his throat as big as a cantaloupe. After Brother and Sister read their poem, it was Lizzy Bruin's turn to say something about her dad. After Lizzy came Cousin Fred. As the cubs read their tributes, Papa thought about all the wonderful moments he had shared with his family. Well, they weren't always wonderful. But they certainly were moments.

Suddenly there was the sound of applause and cheering. It brought Papa back to the here and now of the Papa's Day Surprise. Cubs and mamas were on their feet. It had been a wonderful party and a wonderful Father's Day!

The guests headed for their homes.

"Cubs," said Papa as he drove down the hill to their tree-house home, "I want to thank you for that lovely poem."

“Mama helped us with it,” said Brother.

“Also,” said Papa, “I want to thank you for the Papa’s Day Surprise. It was a wonderful gift.”

“That,” said Sister, “was a gift for *all* the papas. We and Mama have a special gift just for you.”

"Just for me?" said Papa. He pulled to a stop at the tree house. He hurried up the front steps, through the front door, and into the living room.

When he saw what was waiting for him, he could hardly believe his eyes.

"A Bearcalounger!" he cried. "Just what I've always wanted!"

It was a special chair that you could adjust up and down. It was the perfect chair for Papa.

Baby Honey began to cry. She was hungry.

It was *also* the perfect place to feed Baby Honey.

Mama and the cubs watched with big smiles as Papa sat back in his new Bearcalounger and gave Baby Honey her bottle.